The wheels on the bus
go round and round,

All day long...

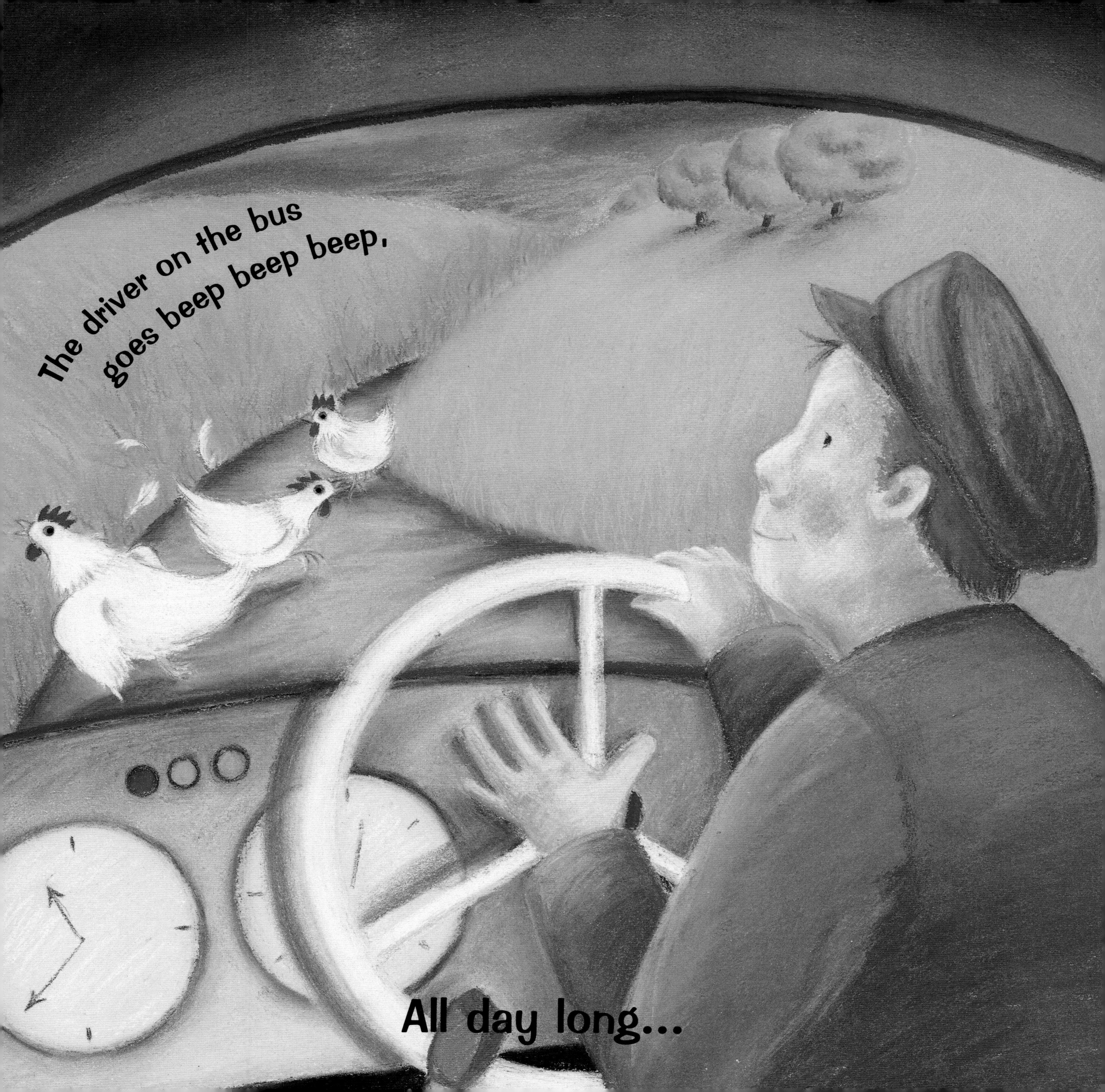

The driver on the bus
goes beep beep beep,

All day long...

The people on the bus
go up and down,

All day long...

The wipers on the bus
go swish, swish, swish,

All day long...

The wheels on the bus
go round and round,
round and round,
round and round,

The wheels on the bus
go round and round,

Until the day is gone!

The wheels on the bus go round and round...

Join in the fun as this all-time favorite children's song is brought to life by Wendy Straw's charming illustrations.

A BROLLY Book

ISBN 978-0-9807307-3-9

9 780980 730739 >

Children's